Folk Tales

Folk Tales from Haryana

JAI NARAIN KAUSHIK

SHIPRA

ISBN: 81-7541-126-0 (HB)
81-7541-184-8 (PB)

Folk Tales from Haryana

First Published in India in 2004

Published by :
SHIPRA PUBLICATIONS
115-A, Vikas Marg, Shakarpur,
Delhi-110092 (India)
Ph. : 22458662, 22500954 Fax : 22458662
Email : info@shiprapublications.com
Website : www.shiprapublications.com

Laser Typesetting by :
R.S. Prints,
New Delhi-110049

Printed at :
Choudhary Offset Process
Delhi-110051

Preface

Children like to listen and read stories. Simple plots full of curiosity are always appreciated by them. The themes related to birds, animals, kings and queens, fairies, fantastic heroes, imaginary worlds etc., are a point of attraction for them. Limited characters with full vigour are praised by them. They enjoy the defeat of deceits and ill characters. The environment of their experience or imagination is liked by them.

The language of these stories should be simple. The sentences should be short representing various structures. The vocabulary should be within the comprehension of the children representing basic vocabulary tending towards language development.

Entertainment, enjoyment, refreshment and development of imagination are the main aims of a story. Instead of direct teaching it should compel the reader to draw his own conclusions.

The 'Folk Tales From Haryana' has been written to cover all the above salient features of a story. It reflects Haryanvi culture, beliefs, disbeliefs, dogmas, imagination, direction, which the parents want to inclucate from generation to generation. There is possibility that some of the stories might cross borders but it only reflects their popularity.

It is hoped that a reader with limited vocabulary will also enjoy this collection. It will enhance his reading taste and comprehension capacity.

C-605, Saraswati Vihar
Delhi-110034, India

Dr. J.N. Kaushik

Contents

1

Moonga and Motha

In olden days there lived two sisters. Their names were Moonga and Motha. They were named after two Indian pulses—Moonga and Motha. They belonged to a poor farmer family.

Once Moonga said to her mother, "Could I visit my maternal grand mother's village? I shall enjoy lot of sweet — meats and funs. I shall return after gaining some weight."

The kind mother laughed and gave her consent.

She started her journey in the morning hours to avoid the heat of the sun.

On her way to grandma's house she came across a horse. The horse neighed to draw Moonga's attention.

Moonga noticed the horse and approached it. She said in an imploring mood, "Dear horse, what sort of help I can do for you? I am on my journey to grandma's house".

The horse said, "My stable is very dirty. Will you kindly sweep it?"

Moonga agreed and swept the stable. The horse thanked her and she proceeded on her journey.

She had hardly covered some distance, she came across a cow. The cow bellowed to draw

Moonga's attention.

Moonga went to the cow and said, "What sort of help I can do for you? I am on my journey to grandma's house".

The cow said, "I have no hay in my manger. I am hungry. Will you kindly arrange some grass for me?"

Moonga agreed and arranged some grass for it. The cow thanked her and she proceeded on her journey.

On her way she came across an old woman also. The woman was weeping. Moonga went to her and said, "What sort of help I can do for you? I am going to my grandma's house."

The old woman said, "I have fever and headache. Will you kindly cook some food for me?"

Moonga agreed and cooked food for the old lady. She blessed her. Moonga proceeded on her onward journey. She got tired but she was happy that she had helped the needy. She never expected anything in return from the horse, cow and old woman.

When Moonga reached maternal grandmother's house she embraced her and wished her a happy life. During her stay she served her grandma. Moonga had lot of sweet-meats and fun.

One day she missed her parents very much. Moonga said, "Grandma, I have enjoyed a lot here. I got love and affection from you. Now I want to go back to my mother."

The grandmother arranged lot of presents and sweets for her. She wished her a happy journey also.

On her way back she came across the same

old lady. She was feeling well that day. The old lady gave many presents to Moonga and wished her a happy return journey.

She had hardly gone few yards when she saw the same cow. The cow felt happy and gave her a pitcher full of milk. Moonga thanked her and proceeded for downward journey.

Moonga was loaded with many presents. The horse saw her. It neighed and came to her. The horse said, "Moonga, you are a very kind girl. You helped me at the time of your onward journey. You kindly sit on my back. Load your presents on me. I shall take you to your home. You must be tired."

Moonga sat on its back and reached her home. She thanked the horse for its kindness.

Moonga's parents were very happy to receive her back with so many presents and sweets.

Motha, the younger sister, felt jealous. She said to her mother, "I shall also go to my grandmother's house."

The mother permitted her too. She proceeded on her journey. Motha first came across the same horse. It asked for her help in cleaning its stable. Motha was in a hurry. She did not oblige the horse.

As she went further she came across the cow. The cow asked her help for collecting some hay for it. Motha was still in a hurry. She did not oblige the cow also.

Next to cow she came across the same old woman. She asked for her help in cooking some food as she was unwell. Motha was in a hurry and did not lend any help to her.

Motha reached her grandma's house. The grandma welcomed her and gave her sweets to eat. Motha never lent a helping hand to the old grand parents. She always said, "I am here just for enjoyment, why should I help you?"

The grandma was fed up with her arrogant behaviour. Motha sensed it and asked for returning to her parents. They did not give any presents to her.

On her back journey to home she came across the old woman. Motha asked for some food. The old woman paid her in the same coin.

She came across the cow and asked for some milk. The cow too did not oblige her. She was thirsty but helpless.

Motha came across the horse. She was badly tired. She asked the horse for a ride. The horse did not oblige her.

Badly tired and hungry she reached her parents. Her parents noticed that she was empty handed. Instead of gaining weight she became very weak.

Motha's mother embraced her out of pity. She began to weep. Her mother told Motha that she was loser due to her unhelpful and arrogant behaviour.

2

The Farmer and the Cock

Once there was a farmer. He had some fields nearby the village. One day he sowed some seeds in his fields.

There lived a cock in a cottage nearby the fields. The cock was very naughty. It was always busy in digging the dirty places in search of insects. Sometime it would sit on some one's head or shoulder. It would not hesitate in riding cats and dogs' back. It thought itself as a king because it had a red crown on its head. The cock was a point of attraction for the street boys.

Once it wanted to change its taste. It was fed-up with insects. It was in search of corn. It went to the nearby fields. It scratched some earth by its nails. It found many sweet corns in earth. It ate to its fill and flew away.

The farmer visited his fields. He was surprised to see that a large part of his field had been scratched out by some bird. He thought that it must be mischief of the naughty cock.

The farmer arranged a trap for the cock. When the cock came to peck the corn the farmer trapped it. He tied its leg with a rope and tucked it to his cot.

The cock saw a bullock cart coming towards it.

The cock crowed to draw the coachman's attention. It said, "Please free me from the clutches of this farmer. I shall arouse you in the early morning."

The bullock cart driver was in a hurry. He said to the cock, "My bullocks are hungry. I have no time. The horseman will come and help you."

The cock saw a horseman coming nearby. The cock crowed to draw his attention. It said, "Kind horseman, please free me from the clutches of this farmer. He will kill me."

The horseman felt pity and said to the farmer, "Please free this cock. You take my horse in its exchange."

The farmer did not agree. The horseman was helpless. He proceeded on his journey.

After some time an elephantrider reached there. The cock crowed to draw his attention. The cock said, "Kind elephantrider, please free me from the clutches of this farmer, he will kill me."

The elephantrider felt pity and said to the farmer, "Please free this cock. You take my elephant in its exchange."

The farmer did not agree. The elephantrider was helpless. He proceeded on his journey.

Fortunately there came a Sadhu with his disciples. The cock saw and crowed to draw their attention. The cock said, "Please free me from the clutches of this farmer. I shall accompany you and arouse you in the early morning. If I am not freed he will kill me."

The Sadhu felt pity on it and said to the farmer, "Please free this cock. I shall ask all my disciples to work on your fields. They will make good the loss caused by this cock."

The Sadhu requested the farmer again and again to free the cock. The farmer did not agree.

The Sadhu became angry. He said to his disciples, "The farmer is very cruel. Beat him with my long stick or cudgel. Free the cock. Cruelty towards birds is a sin."

The disciples beat the farmer. He freed the cock. The cock was happy. It flew and sat on a tree.

The cock mocked at the farmer and said,

"O poor farmer!
You preferred beating by Sadhu's force,
Instead of taking elephant and horse."

3

Camel and Jackal

Once there lived a jackal in a thick jungle. At night it came out in search of food. There were some water-melon fields nearby. It used to eat to its fill. It became very stout.

One night it was roaming on the bank of a river. It saw a camel. The jackal wanted to have a joyride on the back of the camel.

The jackal went to the camel and paid respect by howling. The camel was happy. The camel gurguled to pay back the respect.

The camel said, "Dear jackal, you are very stout. What do you eat? Can I share some lunch with you?"

The jackal said, "Dear camel, I never have my lunch. I always take my dinner. You know, I never come out from my den during daytime. You can have a dinner with me."

The camel said, 'But my belly is big. I am a glutton."

The jackal said, "The water-melons are also of big size. They are full of sweet water. You can quench your thirst and hunger."

The camel was overjoyed. Saliva began to flow from its mouth. It requested the jackal to take him to the water-melon fields as early as possible.

Camel and Jackal

The jackal said, "It is full moonlit night. Your size is big. There is possibility that you may be spotted out by the farmer. Cannot you postpone it for any dark night?"

The camel became restless. It gurguled and said, "I seldom get a free chance to roam about. I shall not miss the dinner with you tonight."

The jackal agreed. It said, "Dear camel, I cannot cross the deep river. You make me sit on your back and cross the river. The water-melon fields are far off from the river."

The camel agreed. The jackal mounted on camel's back. The jackal was happy to enjoy the cool air on camel's back. The camel crossed the river with great care. Both of them reached the fields.

The camel and the jackal started eating the water-melons. The jackal ate one or two melons. The camel was very impatient. It went on eating and eating.

The jackal said, "Dear camel, I am in the habit of howling after taking my food."

The camel said, "Dear jackal, I am still hungry. Do not howl for a while. If you howl the farmer will wake up. I shall be spotted out. He may give me a beating."

The jackal said, "I am helpless, I cannot break my habit for you."

The jackal began to howl. The farmer woke up. He noticed the camel and gave it a good beating. The jackal hid itself behind a bush and remained unnoticed.

When the farmer went away the jackal came out of the bush. It came to the camel. The camel was angry, and full of revenge. It decided to teach him a lesson.

To cross the river the jackal sat on the camel's back again. When the camel reached midstream, it said, "Dear jackal, I am in the habit of dipping and tossing in the water after my dinner."

The jackal said, "It is midstream. The water is deep and gushing. If I fall in the river it will sweep me away. Toss your body at the river bank."

The camel said, "The water at the bank is very shallow. I cannot dip there. Why should I break my habit for you."

The camel dipped in the midstream. The jackal was swept away by the waves. It howled and howled but all in vain. The camel came out from the river and started chewing its cud.

4

Sparrow and a Little Crow

There was a sparrow. A crow became its friend. Once the sparrow found a pearl and the crow a sweet cake. Crow ate it up alone. The crow snatched the sparrow's pearl and sat on a tree. Poor sparrow was sad.

The sparrow said to the tree, "Fly away the crow from your branch. It is a bad crow. It has snatched my pearl."

The tree said, "Why should I ask it to fly away. It has done no harm to me."

The sparrow was sad. It went to a woodcutter and said, "Please cut the tree. The tree is not flying away the crow. The crow has snatched my pearl."

The woodcutter said, "Why should I cut the tree. It has done no harm to me."

The sparrow said, "Won't you cut the tree? I shall see to it."

The woodcutter said, "Yes, you may."

The sparrow was not disappointed. It went to the king and said, 'Please scold and order the woodcutter to cut the tree. The crow which snatched my pearl is sitting on the tree."

The king said, "Why should I scold and order the woodcutter to cut the tree. He has done no harm to me."

The sparrow said, "Won't you?"

The king said, "I won't."

The sparrow went to the queen and said, "Will you kindly be displeased with the king because the king did not order the woodcutter to cut the tree. A crow which snatched my pearl is sitting on the tree."

The queen said, "Why should I be displeased with the king and ask him to order the woodcutter to cut the tree. The king has not done any harm to me."

The sparrow said, "Won't you?"

The queen replied, "I won't."

The sparrow went to a washerman and said, "You do not wash the queen's clothes. She is not asking the king to get the tree cut. A crow which snatched my pearl is sitting on the tree."

The washerman said, "Why shouldn't I wash the queen's clothes? She has not done any harm to me."

The sparrow said, "Won't you?"

The washerman said, "I won't."

The sparrow went to a little mouse and said, "Gnaw the washerman's clothes with your sharp teeth. He is not stopping to wash the queen's clothes. The queen is not asking the king to order the woodcutter to cut the tree. A bad crow which snatched my pearl is sitting on the tree."

The little mouse felt pity on the sparrow. It praised sparrow's courage. The mouse said, "I shall cut washerman's clothes with my sharp teeth."

The washerman became fearful. He said, "I shall stop washing queen's clothes if she is not displeased with the king."

The queen said, “I shall be displeased with the king if he does not order the woodcutter to cut down the tree.”

The woodcutter said, “I shall cut down the tree if the king asks me to do so.”

When the tree saw a woodcutter coming, it began to tremble. It asked the crow to fly away from its shady branch.

It was very hot day. The crow said, “I shall return the sparrow’s pearl. Do not ask me to fly from your branch.”

The tree felt pity on the crow. The crow returned back little sparrow’s pearl. The sparrow was happy because its efforts bore fruit.

❑❑

5

Buffalo and the Sparrow

Once a buffalo and a sparrow became fast friends. The buffalo would spare grains from its manger or threw off fodder for sparrow. It used to protect the sparrow from its horns if some animal or bird attacked it. The sparrow felt itself fully safe in the company of the buffalo.

One day the sparrow was having a joyride on the buffalo's back. A cool wind was blowing. It was in a sportive mood. The sparrow said, "Let us have some sport."

The buffalo said, "You are too small a friend to play with me. What sort of play we can have?"

The sparrow said, "I shall spit some dung on you. You can repeat the same on me."

The buffalo laughed and said, "Do you know its consequences. For me it means nothing but for you it is death."

The sparrow started the game. The buffalo cleaned the spit with its tail. The sparrow flew happily. It sat under the hind legs of the buffalo. The buffalo spit some dung on it. It was hidden under it. It took out its beak from the dung and began to cry. A jackal happened to pass that way.

The sparrow said, "Why do not you take me out from the dung. You can eat me up."

The jackal was happy. It took the sparrow out of the dung and jumped to eat it.

The sparrow said, "Don't you see that I am so dirty. Why don't you wash me."

The jackal agreed and took it to a pond. It gave many dips to the sparrow. The sparrow was neat and clean but wet.

The jackal again jumped on to eat it up. The sparrow said, "Don't you see that my feathers are wet. They will stuff your mouth. Your throat will be choked with wet feathers. Let me dry them. You may eat me afterwards."

The jackal agreed and put the sparrow aside. Its feather got dried in no time.

The jackal again jumped on it but the clever sparrow flew away and sat on the branch of a tree. The jackal was helpless. It felt sorry on its own foolishness.

❐❐

6

Two Sparrows

Once upon a time there were two sparrows. One was male and another female. They lived together near a well. Their main play was hanging on a rope.

The female sparrow was very active. It used to cook food for the male sparrow. They used to take lunch together. The male sparrow was lazy. It was always hungry.

One day the female sparrow arranged some rice and pulse. It prepared hotpotch from rice and pulse. It was a festival for them. The male sparrow was very unrestful. It wanted to eat the dish without any wait.

The female sparrow said, "The hotpotch is very hot. You may parch your beak with hot dish. You please guard the pot. I shall be back soon. I am going to take my bath first. We shall enjoy the dish together.

The female sparrow flew away to take bath. It had many happy dips in the water. Its feathers became wet. It could not fly. It sat on the bank in the sun. It fluttered its feathers to dry them.

The male sparrow waited for some time. It was a cunning and glutton sparrow. It ate up the half share from the pot. The female sparrow did

not return, It ate up the remaining share also. The pot was empty. Its belly was full. It slept within no time.

The female sparrow flew back after some time. The male sparrow was fast asleep. The hotpotch pot was empty. There was not a grain of rice or pulse in the pot.

The female sparrow was angry because it was hungry. It patted the male sparrow with its wings. The male sparrow got up.

The female sparrow said, "Who has eaten the hotpotch from the pot?"

The male sparrow said, "I have not eaten it. I felt asleep. Some visiting creatures might have eaten it up."

The female sparrow said, "I asked you to guard the pot. Why did you sleep? A hungry creature cannot have a sound sleep like you. You must have eaten it up."

The male sparrow said, "I swear by you. I have not eaten the hotpotch."

The female sparrow was very angry. It said, "Don't take false oath. False oath brings death. You should admit your sin. I shall arrange other food for you."

The male sparrow was very foolish. It repeated its ignorance again and again.

The female sparrow said "I shall judge your statement. I shall have a test."

The foolish male sparrow agreed. The female sparrow took a rope of kachcha yarn. It tied its one end with a tree. The other end was hanging in the well.

The female sparrow said, "Hang yourself with

this yarn in the well. If you have eaten up the hotpotch, the yarn would break down."

The male sparrow usually used to hang with this kachcha yarn. It would never break. The foolish sparrow agreed to undergo the proposed hanging test.

As soon as it hung itself with the yarn it broke down. The male sparrow did not know that it has gained weight by eating up the whole hotpotch alone. It fell in the well and suffered for telling a lie.

❑❑

7

Little Mouse and the Sparrow

Once there lived a sparrow and a little mouse. They were fast friends.

One day the mouse said, "Dear sparrow, let us go out for a holy bath in the river Ganga."

The sparrow agreed. They arranged new clothes. They took parched grains for refreshment as midday meal: The sparrow flew while the mouse moved on the sand.

The sparrow saw a caravan of camel. It said to the mouse, "Little mouse, some camels are nearing you. Be away from the path, lest you may be trampled."

The mouse was frightened. It could not move and was trampled in the sand. Its parched grains scattered. Its new clothes became dirty.

When the caravan passed, the mouse cried, "Dear sparrow, please take me out of the sand or I shall die."

The sparrow was very kind. It caught its tail with beak and pulled out the mouse from sand.

The mouse said, "We shall not go to the Ganga. Let us eat plum." The plum bush was thorny. The mouse got stuck in the bush. The sparrow was enjoying the plums.

The mouse cried, "Dear sparrow, take me out

of thorns."

The sparrow caught it by the tail and pulled it out from the bush. The mouse was fed up with the journey and said to the sparrow, "Let us return home."

The sparrow agreed. They had hardly gone few hundred yards the mouse got struck in buffalo's dung. The mouse cried and the kind sparrow again pulled it out by its tail.

The mouse was dirty. It said to the sparrow, "Please help me in washing the dung from my body."

When the mouse was washing its dirt its paw slipped in the water. It cried for help. The sparrow caught it by its tail and pulled it out.

Once the mouse noticed that its maternal uncle was bringing some presents (Sindhara) on the eve of Teej festival. The mouse ran and helped its uncle in carrying that load. The sparrow also flew with the mouse.

The sparrow said to the mouse, "Please show me the presents which your maternal uncle has brought as Teej presents."

The mouse said, "It is just nothing."

The sparrow said, "Dear mouse, you have become unfriendly so soon."

The mouse said "How? You had never been friendly with me."

The sparrow said, "Did not I pull you out from the sand when you were trampled by a camel?"

The mouse said in a light mood, "There was some pain in my spinal cord. I asked the camel to press it gently to remove the pain. Why did you pull me out of sand?"

The sparrow again said, “I pulled you out from the thorny plum bushes. Don’t you remember?”

The mouse said, “I was making holes in my ears for wearing ear-rings. Why did you pull me out of the bush?”

The sparrow again reminded the mouse, “I pulled you out from buffalo’s dung.”

The mouse said, “I was applying a paste on my body. Why did you pull me out from the dung?”

The sparrow said to the thankless mouse, “I pulled you out from the water when you were about to drown.”

The mouse said, “Instead of going to the Ganga, I was taking a holy dip in the pond. Why did you pull me out from the water?”

The sparrow was highly disappointed. When it was about to leave the mouse it saw its own maternal uncle. Its maternal uncle too had brought Teej festival sweets and toys (Sindhara). The sparrow helped its uncle to carry the load to the house.

The mouse noticed the whole scene. It said, “Dear sparrow, please show your toys to me.”

The sparrow said, “You did not show your presents to me. Why should I show you my toys?”

The mouse realised that it has committed a mistake. It said, “Both of us are good friends. I shall share my toys with you and you do the same for me.”

The kind sparrow was pleased with mouse’s behaviour. Both of them exchanged sweets and toys. They became fast friends again.

8

Weaver Bird and the Elephants

Once there was a thick jungle. It was full of datepalm trees. A weaver bird knit its nest on a tree. The female bird laid eggs in it. Soon beautiful chicks or youngones came out from the eggs. The male bird flew out in search of insects. The female bird guarded the chicks.

There was a pond nearby the birds' nest. A female elephant used to pass by the tree. It rubbed its body against the trunk of the tree for scratching.

One day the female bird said to the female elephant, "Please do not rub your body with this tree. My chicks are very tender. They are badly frightened when you shake the tree with your body."

The female elephant did not pay heed to the female bird's request. She came every day and shook the tree by rubbing its huge body.

One day the female bird said, "You are not listening to my request. Upto this time this discord is limited to the females only. If I ask my male companion this discord may take a serious turn."

The female elephant laughed and laughed on the proudy statement of the bird. It rubbed its body more wildly and went away.

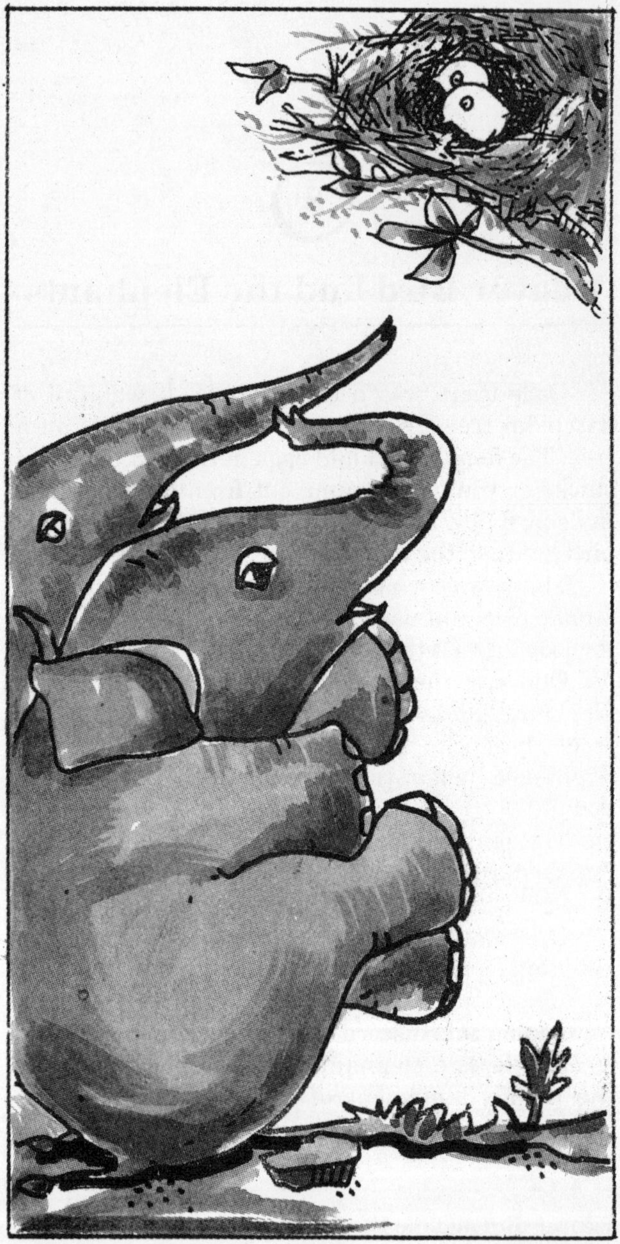

The female elephant talked about the proudy remarks to its male elephant. It laughed.

The next day both the male and female elephants came to that side. Both of them rubbed their bodies against the tree. The male elephant even tried to uproot the tree.

The chicks were badly frightened. The female bird said, "By now I have not told your mischief to my male companion. I have taken great patience. The big and powerful animals should take pity on tiny creatures. We too have our honour and dignity. If we resort to revenge we will teach you a lesson."

The male and female elephants not only ignored but made fun of the bird and went away.

After some time the male bird came with insects in its beak. They enjoyed their lunch. The female bird said in a cool voice, "Dear companion, a female elephant visits our tree every morning, when you are away. It rubs its body with the tree. Our chicks are badly frightened when it shakes it. I requested it not to do so. But it did not agree. Today the male elephant too joined it. They made mockery of small birds."

The male bird was enraged. It said, "Tomorrow we will teach them a lesson."

The two birds made a plan. They whispered in each others ears and laughed. The plan was perfect.

Next day male and female elephants came near to their tree. The male bird said, "We never attack innocents. We never attack first. If you even touch our tree we will not sit silent. There are other trees nearby. You can rub your body there."

The elephants laughed and laughed. They took bird's warning very lightly. Both of them started rubbing their body against that very tree.

Both the birds flew out of their nest. The male bird entered in male elephant's ear and the female in the female's ear. They began to prick their ears from inside. The elephants ran. They could not withstand the severe pain. Both of them fell down on the ground. They stretched their legs upwards.

They folded their legs and prayed for pardon. The birds were very kind. They forgave them. The couple-elephant never came near to their nest. The chicks were happy.

❐❐

9

Illiterate Dogs

Once there lived a male jackal in the jungle. It felt very lonely. It was in search of a companion.

It saw a female jackal. It was happy to see female jackal. The male jackal said, "Dear female jackal, I am alone. My female companion died in some accident. It was my queen. Now I am in search of another queen. Can you offer yourself as my queen?"

The female jackal said, "Only a king has a queen. You are not a king. Do not allure me. I am not so fool to be taken by your words."

The male jackal said, "My dear, do not doubt me. I am really the king of this jungle."

The female jackal said, "Only a lion has the right to be the king of the jungle. You are a jackal."

The male jackal rubbed its tail gently on the body of the female time and again. It said, "Dear female jackal, my queen was badly wounded in saving the lion from a tragic tragedy. The lion was also badly wounded. The lion was so happy with my queen's sacrifice that before dying he made me the king of this jungle."

The female jackal said, "Do not entice or allure me. You are not a king. You cannot protect my offsprings and myself. Have you any proof of being

a king?"

The male jackal said, "Yes, I have."

The female jackal said, "Then show me the proof."

The male jackal took out a piece of paper and said, "My sweet queen, you can see this decree given to me as a dying gift by the lion. You can have it with you permanently."

The female jackal said, "No dear, I have full faith in you now. I am unable to safeguard this decree. I take your words and offer myself to you as a queen."

Both of them rubbed their tails gently with each other. Now she was the queen of that jungle.

Time passed on. The Queen jackal gave birth to little offsprings. It called them prince and princess.

Once they were strolling nearby a village. Some dogs saw their herd. The dogs ran after the jackals. The male jackal noticed the dogs. It said, "Dear queen, let us run away, The dogs are after us. They will kill our offsprings."

The queen objected and said, "Why should we run? You are the king of this jungle. They are simple dogs. They must be coming to bow before us."

The jackal said, "O, no dear no, let us run. Our life is in danger."

The queen jackal said again, "You have the decree of king with you. You can show them. They may read it from this paper."

The king jackal was restless. It said "The dogs of this village are illiterate. They cannot read this decree. Let us hide ourselves in some den."

10

The Warlike and Lion-killer Foxes

Once there lived two foxes. One of them was male and other female. The female fox gave birth to beautiful offsprings.

The male fox went out in search of food. The female fox looked after their offsprings. They were enjoying a happy life.

One day the male fox was out for hunting, It saw a lion. It was frightened, but it took courage. It reached its den with great care.

Incidentally the lion also came to that side. The lion found a suitable den to live in. The foxes could not go out for prey because the lion's den was nearer to them. Their family became to starve.

One day the male fox struck a novel idea in its mind. It said to its female companion, "You call me the 'lion killer' (Singh Pachhar) and I shall call you the 'warlike' (Ranjhanjhni)".

The female fox said, "We cannot become brave simply by changing our names. We are, what we are."

The male fox said, "This is a part of our strategy to keep the lion away from that den." It explained the whole plan.

Next day when the lion came to its den their youngones started crying.

The male fox spoke in a loud voice, "Dear warlike queen, why our youngones are weeping?"

The female fox said, "My Lion-killer king, they are weeping because they are hungry."

The male fox said, "What do they want to eat"?

The female fox said, "They want lion's flesh."

The male fox said, "Yesterday I killed a lion. You must have sufficient flesh by now. Our young-ones have become glutton."

"Dear Lion-killer", said the female fox, "that lion's flesh has become stale. They want fresh flesh."

"Yes I shall just go out for hunting some lion", said the male fox.

The lion heard their conversation. It was frightened. It did not move from its den.

The next day the lion heard the same conversation. It decided to quit that den. It had just moved out of its den, the male fox pushed a huge piece of rock. The stone started rolling. It made a big sound. The lion thought that the 'Warlike' and the 'Lion-killer' are following me. The lion ran very fast and never returned to that jungle again. The male and female foxes lived a happy life for a long time.

11

The Clod and the Leaf

Once there was a farmer. He had dry fields. There were big clods or lump of earth in the fields. There grew an 'Aak' bush. Its leaves were broad in size.

A clod and a leaf became friends. When the fast and stormy wind blew, the leaf flew here and there. Sometimes it flew up and fell down on earth. It became to decay. The clod felt pity on the leaf. The clod said, "How helpless my friend is? But its fate is such."

One day a rainy storm set in. It began to rain. When the rainy showers fell on the clod it began to dissolve. The leaf saw the pitiable condition of its friend. It said, "How helpless my friend is? But its fate is such."

When the rain stopped the clod said to the leaf, "We are friends. We should help each other in the rainy and stormy season."

The leaf said, "We are helpless. How can we help each other?"

The clod said, "When the stormy wind will blow I shall sit on you. You will not be blown up and down by the wind. You will remain unhurt."

The leaf was happy. One day a strong wind blew. The clod sat on the leaf. The wind could do

no harm to the leaf. The leaf said to the clod, "A friend in need is a friend indeed."

One day it began to rain. The rain was very heavy. The showers were very fast. The leaf flew from its place and covered the clod. The showers could do no harm to the clod. The clod was happy. It said to the leaf, "A friend in need is a friend indeed."

They helped each other on several occasions. One day it so happened that a storm was accompanied by rain. The leaf tried to cover the clod. But it was helpless because the wind would not allow it to sit. It blew the leaf away time and again.

The clod tried to sit on the leaf. But the leaf would flew away here and there. The clod started dissolving due to heavy rain. Both the friends were helpless. They shared each other's grief helplessly.

(12)

A Never Lasting Story

Once there was a king. He was very fond of listening stories. He rewarded good storytellers. So, good storytellers used to come from far off places.

Once he announced, "I shall give a lot of money to a person who will relate a never ending story. If the story ends the storyteller will be jailed."

Many storytellers thronged his court to try their luck. The stories or the storytellers never went beyond one week. Many storytellers were defeated in their bid. All of them were jailed. They were very unhappy with the king.

One day a storyteller came and said, "I shall tell a never ending story."

The king said' "Do you know the result if your story ends?"

The storyteller said, "I shall accept the jail gracefully. But if my story never ends I shall not accept cash amount. Kind God has given me enough to eat."

The king said, "Tell me your condition. If acceptable I shall ask you to tell the story."

The storyteller said, "If I tell a never ending story, you shall set free all the storytellers who have been jailed in their venture."

The king agreed and asked him to start telling his story the next day.

The next day came. The king sat in his stately chair. His courtiers were sitting with great patience. The storyteller bowed before the court and took his chair.

The storyteller started telling the story. He said that there was a farmer. He was very hard worker. He ploughed his fields at proper time. He watered his fields properly. He sowed the harvest at proper time. He weeded out the unwanted plants. He sprinkled proper manures at proper time.

Once he sowed bajra or millet crop in his field. The clouds rained at proper time. He ploughed his field properly. The crop was excellent. He winnowed the grains and collected it properly.

The farmer had no gunny bags. He stored the bajra-grains in a big store. The store had a big hole in its wall. Some sparrows flew in through the hole. They noticed bajra-grains. They were happy.

One of the sparrows took some grains in its beak and flew out with a fluttering sound. The next sparrow came. It also took some grains in its beak and came out fluttering from the hole.

The storyteller repeated the sentence, "One sparrow flew in. It took some grains and flew out fluttering from the hole."

The king was fed up with this sentence. He said, "Let us proceed further. What happened next?"

The storyteller said, "Sir, It will take the sparrows years to eat up the whole grains. The farmer will reap the next crop and will store in the same store. The next part of the story will start only when the sparrows have emptied the whole grains".

The king was very much disappointed. The king accepted that the story would never last. He accepted his defeat and freed all the storytellers who were in the prison.

The storyteller was congratulated by all the storytellers for helping their fellow professioners.

13

The Weaver Sparrow and a Monkey

Once there was a weaver sparrow or Baya. It used to knit very beautiful nest. The nest used to swing under a branch of a tree. The nest was very akin to our own house. There were straw-cushions. There were separate rooms for hatching and bedding. The nest was lit with a special light arrangement from some mud and glowing insects.

One day it started raining. The rain was very heavy. The weaver bird flew to its nest. It peeped through the hole of its nest. It enjoyed the cool showers of the rain. The soft air was swinging its nest gently.

In the meanwhile a monkey came to that tree for shelter. It was fully wet. It was shivering badly. It was in search of thick bough. It tried to hid itself in the boughs but it was too big for them.

The weaver bird was looking at the monkey's movements. It was feeling pity on the monkey. It was proud that it could knit such a beautiful nest without hands. The monkey has two hands. It looks like a man and still it cannot make a nest or shelter for itself. The monkey is lazy.

The weaver bird chirped from its nest to draw the monkey's attention. The monkey heard the

The Weaver Sparrow and a Monkey

bird's chirp. It gazed the bird's behaviour.

The weaver bird was so much proud of its nest that it could not help sarcasting the monkey. The bird did not know the monkey's temperament. The bird said,

> "Two hands and human body
> God has bestowed,
> You lazy naughty monkey,
> can't make abode.

The weaver bird repeated this couplet again and again. The monkey became angry. It jumped on the bird's nest. The bird flew away. The monkey tore bird's nest to pieces.

The weaver bird realised its mistake. It felt that it should not have given unwanted advice to an animal like monkey in a sarcasting way. One should not be proud of one's abode.

❏❏

14

Drip-Drop and a Lion

Once there was a washerman. He used to wash the villagers' clothes. He had a small thatched cottage. He used to keep the washed clothes in a safe corner.

The washerman had a donkey. He used to carry dirty clothes on its back. He setfree the donkey for grazing on canal bank.

One day the donkey went far off while grazing. The washerman did not notice it. He brought the washed clothes on his head. His wife and son also shared his load.

The washerman was very sad. His wife said, "Do not be worried. The donkey is after all a donkey. It would feed itself fully and return home by night."

The washerman was restless. He could not sleep till late night. He said to his wife, "I shall go and search out my donkey."

The washerman's wife said, "The night is dark. It is raining outside. A lion visits village-streets occasionally. Are you not afraid of a lion"?

The washerman said, "I am not afraid of lion."

"Are not you?" said the washerman's wife.

"What are you afraid of"? she said again.

"I am afraid of drip-drops (Tapkaa). It is

raining. The roof of our cottage is not in proper order. It may leak. Leaking drip-drops may spoil our washed clothes," said the washerman.

The lion was standing in the back lane. It overheard the conversation between the washerman and his wife. He thought I have never heard the name of Drip-Drop in my life. The Drip-Drop may be stronger than me. It is so because the washerman is not afraid of me. I must leave this place immediately. The lion went away and took shelter in a barn.

The washerman did not care for rain and darkness. He went towards the barn. He was under the impression that the donkey must be grazing there. He spotted a donkey like shade in the barn. He thought if I make a noise it may run away. He went near it and sat on its back. He caught hold it by ears.

The lion was frightened. It thought that the person on its back must be the same Drip-Drop. He is stronger than me, that is why he has the courage to ride me. The lion began to run fast.

The washerman realised his mistake when he noticed that the ears of this animal were smaller than the donkey. Its speed was very fast. It must be a lion. He was afraid but he was helpless.

Both the lion and the washerman wanted to get rid of each other. They were in search of some suitable occasion.

It was dawn. The lion ran through under a tree. The washerman let loose the lion's ears and caught hold the branch of the tree. The lion slipped away from his hold. Both of them had a sigh of relief.

15

A Crazy Crow

Once there was a crow. It used to eat other birds' eggs when they were away from their nests. It would not spare their chickens or nestlings.

Once a sparrow laid four eggs. The crow wanted to eat up the eggs. But the vigilant sparrow never flew away from its nest. The crow became very crazy. It went to the sparrow and said, "Little sparrow, I am very hungry. I want to eat your eggs."

The sparrow was very clever. It said in a polite voice, "My dear crow, my eggs are very beautiful. Your beak is very dirty, better you go and wash your beak."

The crow was pleased. It flew to a well and said, "Dear well, I want water to wash my beak. Please give me some water."

The well said, "Crow never washes its beak. Why do you want to wash your beak?"

The crow said, "I wanted to eat a sparrow's eggs. It said that your beak was dirty, go and wash your beak. If I wash it the sparrow will allow me to eat its eggs."

The well understood the sparrow's cleverness and crow's folly. The well said, "Dear crow, you bring a pitcher. I shall fill it with water. You may wash your beak and eat the sparrow's eggs."

The crow flew away and went to a potter. The crow said, “Dear potter, you give me a pitcher. I shall fill it from the well. I shall wash my beak and the sparrow will allow me to eat its eggs.”

The potter was very clever. He understood the crow’s craziness. The potter said, “Dear crow, I have no digging instrument to dig the earth. You go and bring the instrument.”

The crow flew away. It went to an ironsmith and said, “Dear ironsmith, you give me a digging instrument. The potter will dig earth to make a pitcher for me. The well will fill it with water. I shall wash my beak. The sparrow will allow me to eat its eggs.”

The ironsmith was very clever. He understood the whole story. He gave the crow a blunt digging instrument. It was very hot. The crow put it on its feathers. Some of its feathers burnt.

The crow took the digging instrument to the potter. The potter dug out some sand. He made a small hole in the bottom of the pitcher.

The crow took the pitcher to the well. The well did not fill the pitcher to its full. The crow could not wash its beak because the water leaked out from the hole.

The crow flew to the sparrow’s nest with dirty beak. When the crow reached the sparrow’s nest it found that there was not even a single egg in the nest. Four beautiful little sparrows were sitting on a branch with their mother. The crow was very much disappointed. The crow pounced upon the sparrows. All the sparrows showered peck with their beaks on the crow. The crow flew away and disappeared. He never came to them again.

16

Revengeful Animals

Once there was a jackal in a jungle. It lived with the members of its family. One day a lion and lioness happened to pass by its den. The lioness was very hungry. It killed the jackal's offsprings and ate them up. The jackal was helpless. It decided to take revenge from the lion.

The lioness was pregnant. It was in search of a den for its cubs. The jackal said to the lioness, "Respected queen, you have no cave for your would be cubs. You can use my den. I have no child. I shall play with your cubs for my entertainment."

The lioness agreed. The lioness was long and thin. It managed to enter the jackal's den. It gave birth to three beautiful cubs.

The jackal sit outside the den. The lion was out for hunting at that time. When the lion returned the jackal congratulated it. The lion was happy. It wanted tö see little cubs. The entrance of the den was narrow. It was difficult for the lion to enter the den.

The jackal said, "What an unfortunate father you are. You cannot see the face of your children. Take courage. Put your head inside the hole and make a forceful push. The den is very broad from inside. Your little cubs are calling you."

The lion became very passionate. It put its head in the cave and tried to push itself inside with great force. Its face was very broad. It got struck inside the hole. Its throat got chocked and it died in no time.

The jackal invited other animals. They ate up the lion as a great feast. It took its revenge and felt happy.

The lioness was sad. It thought a plan to kill the jackal. It prayed to jackal, "Dear jackal, now I am a widow. How can I spend my life without a male companion. Let us be married. You look after my cubs."

The jackal accepted the proposal. One day the lioness said, "Dear jackal, my cubs never go outside the den. They must learn the art of hunting. Take them outside. Let them have some risk. Teach them thc art of jumping ditches and wells."

The jackal agreed. It took the cubs near a well. It asked the cubs to jump across the well time and again. The cubs were very active. They jumped across the well again and again.

After some practice one of the cubs said, "Dear uncle, we have made ample practice. You also jump across the well. There must be some novelty in your jumps. We shall observe you."

The jackal agreed hesitatingly. It tried to jump across the well. The jackal had become very weighty by eating the lion's flesh. It fell down in the well and died.

The cubs returned to the lioness. They told about the jackal's death inside the well. The lioness became happy. It told the cubs about their father's killing by the jackal. The cubs too were happy.

17

Lioness Married to a Jackal

Once there lived a lion and lioness. They had a female cub, named Rani. When Rani, the female cub, grew up they wanted to marry it to a suitable match.

Once the couple was roaming in the jungle. Rani was with their parents. They saw a jackal jumping over an elephant again and again. They were surprised to see that scene.

The lion went to the jackal and said, "Who killed this elephant?"

The jackal said, "I killed it in an encounter. It challenged my authority over this part of the jungle."

The lion was impressed by the bravery of the jackal. The lion said to the lioness, "Dear queen, we have found a suitable match for our daughter, Rani. I shall marry Rani with this jackal."

First of all Rani objected to that marriage and questioned jackal's bravery. But like an obedient daughter she agreed.

The lion said to the jackal, "Come to our den with your marriage party. It should be large enough. Come with pomp and show. We shall give you a warm welcome."

The jackal went for marriage alone. The lion

asked, "Why have you come all alone? Where are other members of the marriage party?"

The jackal said, "The river was in spate. All of them have been washed away. They were timid and weak. I was the bravest who crossed the river."

The lion was satisfied with his reply. Rani and jackal were married. Rani and jackal became husband and wife.

Once Rani went to drink water in a river. The jackal was with her. The jackal also entered the flowing water to prove its bravery. The lioness withstood the flow but the jackal was washed away by the gushing water. The lioness saw the accident and saved the jackal.

The lioness said, "Dear jackal, I am not a befitting match for you. I shall divorce you. You are so weak that you cannot protect yourself. How can you protect me in the time of need?"

The jackal said, "Dear queen, I was just scaling water. I know different types of swimming. Being a woman you got frightened just for nothing."

One day they were roaming by a village. Some dogs spotted the jackal. The dogs ran after the jackal. The jackal ran away and returned after a long time.

The lioness said, "You are a timid fellow. Why did you run away when the dogs barked at you?"

The jackal said, "They were my relatives. They wanted to have some private talk about my married life. I took them away in the jungle and had a talk with them."

One night a herd of jackal was howling in a nearby lake. The jackal heard their howling. It could not remain without howling. It began to howl with other jackals. The lioness noticed it. It was confirmed that the jackal was after all a timid jackal. Rani lioness was not a match for it.

Rani was highly enraged. It jumped over the jackal and killed it mercilessly. Rani, the lioness, returned to its parents and related the whole story to them .

❐❐

18

The Revengeful Fox

Once there was a fox. It gave birth to two cubs. Its male companion died in some accident. It missed the male companion so much that it became very weak. It could not feed its cubs properly. They too became very weak.

There lived a jackal couple near by. They always noted the movements of the fox's family. Once the fox said to this jackal couple, "I and my cubs are helpless in the absence of my male companion. Kindly look after them when I am away for hunting."

The jackal couple nodded and assured the fox for all sort of help.

Once the fox was away for hunting. The cubs were playing with each other in a hunting mood. The jackal couple felt hungry. They pounced upon the cubs and ate them up. Even a small bone was not spared.

When the fox returned, it searched for the cubs. But they were no more on this earth. The jackal couple was fast asleep in a shadowy bush. The fox made groaning noise. The jackal couple opened their eyes. The fox asked about its cubs. The couple showed their ignorance and said, "Now they are quite grown up. They must be out for hunting."

The jackal couple yawned and slept again. The fox smelt their breath. It became sure that the jackals had eaten up its young ones. The fox was helpless. It decided to take revenge.

One day the fox met a wolf. The wolf was old and weak. The fox said, "Dear uncle, you have become so weak. Are you not keeping good health?"

The wolf said, "I am old now. I cannot run. So I cannot prey also. Can you help me in this old age?"

The fox smiled and said, "You had been the protector of this jungle. You take rest in your den. I shall arrange for your prey".

The old wolf became very happy. The fox returned to its burrow. The jackal couple was still yawning. The fox said to the jackal, "I met a wolf yesterday. He is the protector of this jungle. He wants to demarcate separate land for each animal for hunting. None will intrude in any one's territory henceforth. He has full record of the land. He has invited both of you for allotting a separate piece of land. Avail your first chance. I have recommended a good piece of land for you.

The jackal couple was highly pleased. They followed the fox and reached the wolf's den. The fox said, "Dear jackal, wolf is my elder brother-in-law. I cannot talk face to face with him. We maintain 'parda system'. You enter the den and ask for your territory".

The jackal agreed and entered the wolf's den. The wolf was ready for its prey. He caught hold the jackal by its ears and pulled it down to the deep den. For a long time the jackal did not turn out. There was some rumbling sound. The fox said,

"The wolf and the jackal must be busy in folding and unfolding the land record. The sound resembles like removing the old record from one place to another."

The female jackal became restless. The fox said, "After all property matters are not solved so easily. It is a question of generations. You go inside and help your companion. I am sorry, I cannot go bare mouthed. You kindly go inside and help in settling the dispute".

The female jackal agreed and pushed its mouth inside the den. The wolf caught hold it by ears and took into the deep den. The wolf enjoyed a double feast.

The fox was happy. It went to the jackal's cubs. It lulled and allured the young ones one by one and took them to a thick bush. The fox also enjoyed a double feast.

19

Worker Sparrow and Shirker Crow

Once there was a crow. It was always hungry. It never worked hard and used to depend upon others.

Once the crow met a sparrow. The crow said to the sparrow, "Let us have common farming. We shall plough and reap the fields together. We shall divide the products in two equal shares."

The sparrow was very hard worker. It accepted the crow's proposal.

Next day the sparrow got up before dawn and said to the crow, "Let us go to the field to cut the bushes before ploughing".

The crow was shirker and not a good worker. It said to the sparrow:

Dear sparrow you go alone,
I shall arrange some food at home.
I cannot work without my smoke,
Do not take it as a joke.

The sparrow was helpless. It went to the field. It removed away the thorny bushes. The field was ready for ploughing. The crow did not reach the field.

The sparrow returned in the late evening.

Next day the sparrow said to the crow, "I have cut the thorny bushes all alone. The fields are ready for sowing the crop. You accompany me to the fields".

The crow said again:

Dear sparrow you go alone,
I shall arrange some food at home.
I cannot work without my smoke,
Do not take it as a joke.

The little sparrow felt pity on the lazy crow and went to the fields alone. It sowed the Bajara or millet crop. The crow did not turn up even that day.

Next day the sparrow said to the crow, "Dear partner, I have sown the crop. Let us go and look after it, otherwise the birds will do harm to the seeds".

The crow was very lazy and cunning. It said,

"Dear sparrow you go alone,
I shall arrange some food at home.
I cannot work without my smoke,
Do not take it as a joke.

The little sparrow was helpless. It pitied its co-partner. It flew to the fields daily. It looked after them till the sun set. It watered the fields alone.

Now the crop was ready for harvesting. The sparrow said to the crow, "My dear crow, the crop is ready for harvesting. Let us go together and reap the fields".

The crow said:

Dear sparrow you go alone,
I shall arrange some food at home.
I cannot work without my smoke,
Do not take it as a joke.

The little sparrow went to the fields. It harvested the crop.

Next day the sparrow went to the crow and said, "I waited for you yesterday. You did not turn up. I cut the crop all alone. Today we shall separate the corn from the chaff. This will be the last item of our cooperative work."

The crow said:

Dear sparrow you go alone,
I shall arrange some food at home.
I cannot work without my smoke,
Do not take it as a joke.

The little sparrow waited for the crow. The crow did not turn up. The sparrow separated the corn from the chaff all alone. It was badly tired.

The sparrow went to the crow next day and said, "Dear co-partner, I have separated the corn from the chaff. Let us go to the fields and divide the product in two equal parts".

The crow was very happy. It flew with the sparrow to the fields. The crow said, "My dear sparrow you are very generous. You have already made two heaps, one of corn and the other of chaff. I opt for corn. You can take chaff for yourself."

The sparrow was very sad. It said to the crow, "This is no justice. I laboured hard and you want to enjoy the gains. God will punish you."

The crow became angry. It threatened to kill the sparrow. The sparrow was helpless.

Suddenly, it began to rain. The rain was followed by a hail-storm. The little sparrow took shelter under the chaff. The crow could not hide itself in the corn. The crow was hit by the hails again and again. It died near the heap of the corn.

The rain stopped. The sparrow came out of the chaff. It felt pity to see the dead crow by the heap of the corn. It collected its corn and enjoyed it for a long time.

20

A Wise Donkey and a Foolish Lion

Once a lion lived in a jungle. It was very proud of its strength. It defeated or killed many wild animals.

One day it was roaming in a jungle. It saw a strange animal with long ears and bushy tail. It had hoofs instead of paws. Its braying voice was strange to the lion.

The lion roared and said, "Who are you?"

The donkey brayed and said, "Who are you?"

The lion said, "I am the king of this jungle. I am strong."

The donkey said, "If you are a strong animal I am the strongest".

The lion said, "Are you?"

The donkey said, "Yes, I am".

The lion roared and said, "Can you have a bout or trial of strength with me?"

The donkey said, "Yes, I accept your challenge".

The lion said, "Be prepared. I shall attack you first."

The donkey said, "I am on fast for the last weak. I have become weaker. We shall have a bout after a week at this very place."

The lion agreed and both of them had their

own path. The donkey became very thoughtful.

It went to a muddy ditch. It rolled there again and again. It added some mud on its body. It went to the dry sand and rolled there time and again. It added some more sand on its body.

The donkey continued this practice for a week. It wrapped enough mud around its body. It grazed green grass every day. It looked very fatty.

The donkey reached the appointed place on the seventh day. The lion was already waiting for the bout.

The donkey said, "You can have your first chance in the trial of strength."

The lion said, "I agree to take my chance".

The lion roared. It stretched its powerful paws and jumped on the donkey. The donkey had several layers of mud on its body. The lion's paws could not touch the donkey's body. Its paws slipped and it came down on the earth with a thud. The lion had never experienced such a slip. It began to pant.

The donkey said, "Mr. Lion, you have tried your strength. Now it is my turn. I shall count up to ten. If you do not stand up you will have to accept your defeat."

The lion took courage. It stood up with great pain. It was still trembling. The donkey went near the lion and said, "Be ready. I am trying my strength on you."

The donkey raised its hind legs with full strength and kicked the lion's mouth with sharp hoofs. It kicked time and again and counted only one attack.

The lion fell down on the earth with broken

teeth and bleeding mouth. It said, "Mr. Donkey, if this is your one attack, I cannot face other attack. I accept my defeat. If I am strong you are the strongest animal of this jungle".

The donkey felt happy and roamed in the jungle fearlessly over a number of years.